Ladybird Readers

A Fight with Underbite

Picture words

Russell

Denny

Autobots

Bumblebee

Optimus
Prime

Sideswipe

Strongarm

Fixit

Grimlock

Underbite
(a Decepticon)

Cybertron

scrapyard

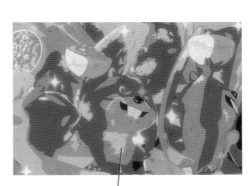

metal

spaceship

quarry

5

Bumblebee was a police robot in Cybertron. He worked with another police robot called Strongarm.

"I'm very happy that you worked with the great Optimus Prime," Strongarm told him. "Optimus was very important to me!"

Optimus Prime was dead. It made Bumblebee sad to think about him, so he didn't answer.

Sideswipe was a fast robot.
At that moment, he was driving
too fast around Cybertron.

"Stop going so fast!"
shouted Strongarm.

But Bumblebee wasn't thinking about Sideswipe. Suddenly, he could see Optimus's face in some water.

"You must go to Earth, Bumblebee!" Optimus told him. "The people there need you!"

Bumblebee used a space bridge to travel to Earth. He didn't know Strongarm and Sideswipe were following him until he arrived there.

"It's my job to stay with you,"
Strongarm said.

"Go back to Cybertron!"
Bumblebee told them.

"No, we won't!" Sideswipe said,
and he ran away.

A few minutes later, Bumblebee and Strongarm met a small robot called Fixit. He was happy to see them.

"I was taking two hundred Decepticons to Cybertron, but our spaceship fell to Earth," Fixit told them. "All the Decepticons ran away!"

Bumblebee was worried. "We have to find those Decepticons and stop them from hurting the people on Earth," he told Strongarm.

At the same time, Russell was helping his dad, Denny, in his scrapyard.

Russell hated the scrapyard. It was boring, and he never had any adventures there.

Suddenly, there was a very loud sound from over in the trees.

"What was that?" Russell asked.

He walked into the forest to find out.

In the forest, Russell saw Sideswipe. He felt very frightened, because he was meeting a robot for the first time!

Sideswipe was afraid, too, because he was meeting a boy for the first time!

But when Underbite suddenly came around the rocks, they were both much more afraid of him!

Underbite was one of the Decepticons from Fixit's spaceship. He was very BIG and very ANGRY.

"I eat metal to get strong," he said. "Once, I ate a whole city!"

When Sideswipe and Russell started to run, Underbite followed them. Then, Sideswipe suddenly changed into a car. Russell was very surprised!

"I eat metal, remember?" Underbite said, when he saw the car.

Russell jumped in and Sideswipe quickly drove away.

The other Autobots saw Underbite, too! They changed into cars and quickly drove back to Fixit's spaceship. Underbite was very strong and they could not fight him.

When they all arrived back at the spaceship, Fixit was happy to see them. But he was not happy to see Underbite! to see Underbite!

"Quick, hide!" Bumblebee told Russell. "Fixit! Stay with him!"

Then, all the Autobots began to fight Underbite.

At that moment, Grimlock woke up.

Grimlock was another bad robot from the spaceship. Now, he wanted to fight Underbite and help the Autobots.

But Underbite saw Denny's scrapyard through the trees.

"Look at all that lovely metal! I feel hungry!" he said, and he started running toward it.

"Oh no! My dad's in the scrapyard!" Russell told the Autobots. "We have to stop Underbite!"

Underbite arrived at the scrapyard.
Grimlock still wanted to fight
Underbite, so he followed him there.

Denny was listening to music while
he moved some old metal toys,
so he didn't see Underbite and
Grimlock fighting near him.

Russell, Bumblebee, Strongarm, and Sideswipe hurried to the scrapyard. There, Strongarm tried to fight Underbite, too.

She made Underbite very angry, and he ran after her and Bumblebee.

Russell quickly found his dad.
Denny was very surprised when
he saw the Transformers.

"A . . . talking robot!" he said.

"All of you, go and hide in a safe place," Bumblebee said. "You too, Strongarm."

"But I don't want to hide," said
Strongarm. "Optimus taught
you to fight. Please teach me
to fight, too."

Underbite and Grimlock were still fighting.

Underbite picked up Grimlock and threw him through the air.

Then, Underbite looked up and saw a city only a few miles away.

"That place is full of metal that I want to eat!" he shouted.

He changed into a car and drove to the city.

"Underbite is very dangerous!" said Strongarm. "There are lots of people in that city. We have to save them!"

Strongarm, Grimlock, and Denny wanted to go with Bumblebee.

"All right," Bumblebee agreed. "But they mustn't know you are a robot, Strongarm. Change into a car that humans drive."

So Strongarm changed into a blue police car, Bumblebee changed into a yellow car, and Denny got in his car, too. They went after Underbite.

The Autobots stopped Underbite
at the city bridge.
He couldn't get into the city to
eat the metal, and he began to
feel hungry and tired.

Then, Sideswipe and Russell arrived with lots of metal toys that Underbite wanted to eat!

Russell and Sideswipe drove the toys away from the city. Underbite followed them.

Russell had an idea. "I know! Let's go to the quarry," he said.

When Underbite tried to eat the metal toys, everyone drove into him, and tried to push him into the quarry.

But Underbite ate some of the metal toys and became strong again!

Then, he picked up Denny, who was still in his car!

Suddenly, help arrived at the quarry. It was Bumblebee's friend, Optimus Prime!

Optimus threw Underbite to the bottom of the quarry.

Then, he picked up Denny's car, and took it to Russell. Finally, Denny was safe!

39

Bumblebee was very happy to see his friend. "I thought you were dead, Optimus!" he said.

"I can't stay on Earth for long," Optimus told him. "You have some good friends now, and you are very strong. There is important work to do here. You can all do it together."

And with those words, Optimus left.

The Autobots decided to
live at the scrapyard with
Denny and Russell. It was
a good place to hide.

"Can I stay with you?" Grimlock
asked. "I want to help, too."

"Yes, you can stay with us,"
Bumblebee told him. That made
Grimlock very happy!

"Perhaps Optimus is right," thought Bumblebee. "Maybe we CAN save Earth from the Decepticons—and have many great adventures, too!"

Activities

The key below describes the skills practiced in each activity.

Spelling and writing

Reading

Speaking

? Critical thinking

Preparation for the Cambridge Young Learners Exams

1 **Look and read. Choose the correct words and write them on the lines.**

scrapyard   quarry   spaceship   metal

1 Cars are made of this.   metal

2 Something that can carry you through space.   ....

3 A place where you can get stones.   ....

4 A place where there is a lot of old metal.   ....

45

2 Look and read. Put a ✓ or a ✗ in the boxes. 📖 ⬡

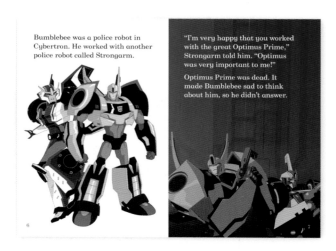

Bumblebee was a police robot in Cybertron. He worked with another police robot called Strongarm.

"I'm very happy that you worked with the great Optimus Prime," Strongarm told him. "Optimus was very important to me!"

Optimus Prime was dead. It made Bumblebee sad to think about him, so he didn't answer.

1 Bumblebee worked alone. ✗

2 Bumblebee and Strongarm worked in Cyberspace. ☐

3 Strongarm didn't want to work with Bumblebee. ☐

4 Optimus Prime was very important to Strongarm. ☐

5 Bumblebee felt happy when he thought about Optimus Prime. ☐

Find the words.

dieghspaceshipeidcjmetalcidkenquarryeichtcarwixhcoptcitydudhescrapyardeotjco

spaceship

scrapyard

metal

quarry

city

car

4 **Complete the sentences.**
Write a—d. 📖

1 Bumblebee used
a space bridge   d

2 He didn't know that

3 Strongarm's job was

4 Bumblebee told
Sideswipe

a to go back to Cybertron.

b to stay with Bumblebee.

c Strongarm and Sideswipe
were following him.

d to travel to Earth.

5 Look and read. Write *yes* or *no*.

At the same time, Russell was helping his dad Denny in his scrapyard.

Russell hated the scrapyard. It was boring, and he never had any adventures there.

Suddenly, there was a very loud sound from over in the trees.

"What was that?" Russell asked.

He walked into the forest to find out.

14

15

1 Russell helps Denny at the scrapyard.

yes

2 There is a lot of old metal at the scrapyard.

....

3 Denny knows what the noise is.

....

4 The scrapyard is close to a forest.

....

6 Circle the correct pictures.

1 Who was dead?

a   b

2 Who was bored at the scrapyard?

 a    b

3 Who uses a space bridge?

 a    b

4 Who followed Bumblebee to Earth?

 a    b

7 Choose the best answers.

1 Underbite was a Decepticon from
   a Earth.
   b Fixit's spaceship.

2 He was a
   a big, angry robot.
   b small, happy robot.

3 He wanted to eat metal to get
   a weak.
   b strong.

4 Russell was
   a more scared of Underbite
     than Sideswipe.
   b more scared of Sideswipe
     than Underbite.

8 **Read the answers. Write the questions.**

When Sideswipe and Russell started to run, Underbite followed them. Then, Sideswipe suddenly changed into a car. Russell was very surprised!

"I eat metal, remember?" Underbite said, when he saw the car.

Russell jumped in and Sideswipe drove away quickly.

The other Autobots saw Underbite, too! They changed into cars and quickly drove back to Fixit's spaceship. Underbite was very strong and they could not fight him.

19

1   What did Sideswipe change into?

Sideswipe changed into a car.

2

Russell felt surprised.

3

Underbite eats metal.

4

He drove away quickly.

9 Circle the correct words.

1 Sideswipe, Bumblebee, and Strongarm changed into **robots. /(cars.)**

2 They met Fixit back at the **spaceship. / city.**

3 **All / None** of the Autobots began to fight Underbite.

4 Grimlock wanted to **eat / fight** Underbite.

10 **Match the two parts of the sentences.** 📖

1 If Bumblebee goes to Earth,

2 If Russell goes to the forest,

3 If Sideswipe and Strongarm follow Bumblebee to Earth,

4 If the Autobots can't find the Decepticons,

a Bumblebee won't be happy.

b they will hurt the people on Earth.

c he will mee Sideswipe.

d he will be able to help the people.

11 Look at the pictures and tell the story to a friend. Use the words and phrases in the box. 🗨 ✿

hurried   surprised   didn't see
followed   fight   scrapyard   Denny
working and listening to music
Russell and the Autobots

Grimlock followed Underbite to the scrapyard . . .

12 **Write the correct sentences.**

1 met • and • Bumblebee • a • robot • called • small • Strongarm • . • Fixit

Bumblebee and Strongarm met a small robot called Fixit.

2 spaceship • Fixit's • was • Decepticons • Underbite • one • . • the • from • of

....

....

3 changed • suddenly • Sideswipe • Then, • car • . • into • a

....

....

56

13 Write *up* or *through*.

1 Underbite picked ⎯⎯ up ⎯⎯ Grimlock.

2 He threw Grimlock ⎯⎯⎯⎯⎯⎯ the air.

3 Underbite saw Denny's scrapyard ⎯⎯⎯⎯⎯⎯ the trees.

4 Then, he looked ⎯⎯⎯⎯⎯⎯, and saw a city close by.

14 Read the questions.
Write complete answers.

1 Why did Underbite drive to the city?

Because there was a lot
of metal there.

2 Why did Strongarm change into
a police car?

3 Why did Underbite feel hungry
and tired?

58

15 **Read the text. Write some words to complete the sentences.**

> The Autobots stopped Underbite at the city bridge. Russell and Sideswipe arrived with lots of metal toys. They knew that Underbite wanted to eat them. Underbite followed Russell, Sideswipe, and the toys away from the city.

1 The Autobots stopped Underbite at _the city bridge_ .

2 Then, Russell and Sideswipe arrived with _____ .

3 Underbite wanted to eat the toys, so he followed Russell and Sideswipe

_____ .

16 Circle the correct pictures.

1 Where did Russell and Sideswipe take Underbite?

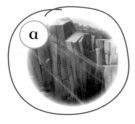  

2 What did Underbite want to eat there?

 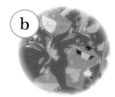 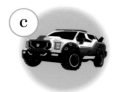

3 Who did Underbite pick up?

4 Who arrived to help at the quarry?

Suddenly, help arrived. It was Bumblebee's friend, Optimus Prime!

Optimus threw Underbite to the bottom of the quarry.

Then, he picked up Denny's car and took it to Russell. Finally Denny was safe!

38

.... Suddenly, Optimus Prime arrived!

.... Denny was finally safe.

1 Underbite picked up Denny in his car.

.... Optimus Prime picked up Denny's car, and took it to Russell.

.... Optimus Prime threw Underbite to the bottom of the quarry.

18 **Ask and answer the questions about the story with a friend.** 💬 ❓

1 *Who saved Denny?*

Optimus Prime saved Denny.

2 How did Bumblebee feel when he saw Optimus Prime?

3 How long could Optimus Prime stay on Earth?

4 Where did the Autobots decide to live?

5 Why did they decide to stay there, do you think?

19 Look at the letters.
Write the words.

1 (y c d s a r p r a)

Grimlock wanted to stay with the
Autobots at the ….. scrapyard ….. .

2 (y t s a)

Bumblebee said that Grimlock could

…………………………………………………… .

3 (c e t p D c i n o s e)

Bumblebee wants to save Earth
from the ……………………………………………… .

4 (v u s a n e d t r e)

Bumblebee also wants to have many
great ……………………………………………………… .

Level 4

The Pied Piper of Hamelin

978–0–241–25378–6 ☐

The Wizard of Oz

978–0–241–25379–3 ☐

Sam and the Robots

978–0–241–25380-9 ☐

The Little Mermaid

978-0-241-29874-9 ☐

Space

978–0–241–25381–6 ☐

Pinocchio

978–0–241–28430–8 ☐

Alice in Wonderland

978–0–241–28431–5 ☐

Under the Oceans

978-0-241-29888-6 ☐

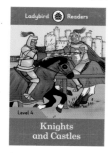

Knights and Castles

978–0–241–28432–2 ☐

Heidi

978–0–241–28433–9 ☐

Peter and the Wolf

978–0–241–28434–6 ☐

Dangerous Journeys

978-0-241-29891-6 ☐

A Fight with Underbite

978-0-241-29890-9 ☐

Sideswipe Loses his Head

978-0-241-29889-3 ☐